SAY
AUDREY II

AARON AKRAM

Charleston, SC
www.PalmettoPublishing.com

First Edition

Paperback ISBN: 979-8-8229-3115-2

Preface: This is not a book to understand, it's one to feel. Not everything needs to make sense. It's a work of imagination and that alone will guide you. All dream sequences should be read out loud. See italics.

For Brian Welsh (who taught me to speak up)

CHAPTERS

PART I

GRADUATION

I fall asleep to remember you, It's all I have anymore.
A vague impression where I lay. The summer never sits so high.
Rocking gently, lost without me, I simply can't fail this time.
Turning over something, the same face I see. Years and
years go by. Still I feel you're out there. Rocking gently,
lost without me, I simply can't fail this time.

There are things above our understanding, the animal nature of man, so far as we achieve we are not immune. We sink in petty things, pride, resentment, competition, discomfort. Small things lead to hatred, anger, war, and fear. We have to stop them before they start. Dissipate the energy with faith and exercise, efforts to control the mind and body, education to know ourselves and why we do what we do, why we feel certain things. Awareness will repay itself. Loving kindness will take us there.

These are the things he learned as a child and saw as a man. Experience in the world was something Audrey always wanted, now he had. "How do we build on this?" he thought, "How far do I take myself? What is enough? What is more than that? Where am I?" Audrey closed his eyes and thought. Today was graduation day. His mother had arranged a party. All his friends would be there. It was a day to celebrate, everything he worked for was complete. There's always further to go and yet he arranged himself to take it in. Days like this don't always come. "I'm happy" he thought, "I love myself for what I've done. I still don't know how I did it." He smiled to himself. He walked upstairs. He was already dressed in a bright yellow shirt and dark jeans. He picked up some books from his room and wondered how the time flew. Always.

When he came back down again, the party had started. The room was crowded. Standing in the corner was a slender girl with black hair. He had to look at her a few times. "Teller? I almost didn't recognize you." They hadn't met for years and she looked amazing. It seemed like every eye was glancing at her and she didn't seem to notice or care, because she was there for him. She wore a black dress with a pink bow around her waist. How she filled that dress he thought. Everything about her carefully pruned. Her face lit with her eyes colored like the beauty he always knew her to be. The way she talked as if a day hadn't gone by. She moved so gracefully, mature, as if she were born that way. A real lady she had become. Fine. Wise. Unassuming and pure. Untouched.

"How is everything? Where are you these days?" asked Audrey.

"I started living in Redding after college and I've been teaching for the last few years. What about you?"

"I just graduated from med school, as you know. It's why we're here today." He said laughing. "How's teaching? You like it? I can see you doing that. I'm sure the kids love you."

"Yeah, I love it. I love them. I'm totally happy right now. For once in my life I guess. So what's next for you?"

"I'm not sure right now. Maybe go off on one last adventure."

"That sounds like you." she said, "Maybe I can join you this time."

Audrey laughed.

"Maybe I could use the company."

They talked like this for a while.

"You have other guests. Go," she finally said. "I'll be waiting here for you."

Audrey went to mingle with them. So many friends of the family were there.

"Remember when you wanted to be a filmmaker?" a friend asked, "What made you want to do that?"

"I remember riding in the car with my parents. I felt safe, like nothing could harm me. I felt peace, joy. We listened to the radio as I stared out the window I would imagine so many things. It was like watching movies. It was my life though. I think everything I see I see that way. This is one big film. All your memories are scenes. You watch them over again. All your dreams too, expressions of you, flights. Abstract parts you never understand. It's a beautiful thing."

"Always a dreamer," he laughed.

They ate and talked. At the end of the night he went back to her. Most of the guests were gone. It was nice to see everyone he said to himself. Some days he felt alone, but now he saw there were so many who loved him. He was whole again.

"I hope you had a good time," he said to her.

"It's not over." She smiled and grabbed his hand. He blushed. "There's so much you have to tell me."

"And you the same," he said.

They sat on the couch next to each other. He had been absent for so long. All these years later, he never knew what he was missing. He offered her tea. They sat quietly and spoke softly.

"I wish Told were here." He said.

"I know. He was so proud of you. You did it Audrey. Everything you said you would."

"At what cost though? I left behind a lot of people. I hurt so many."

"People forgive."

"But I won't forgive myself. Not that easily."

"Today was a good day, wasn't it? Whether you're happy or not is your choice. Remember when all you wanted was to take care of your father. Now you can. You have everything you need. It's all in there." She touched her finger to his head.

"I think you're right. I have the power to do good now. There's a lot of people who need my help. It's up to me."

"You're not Superman." Teller laughed.

"Maybe I could be." He smiled. "I was thinking we should all live as ambassadors to our people. It only takes one person to change the whole way we see a race, a gender, a culture."

"I was thinking about the kids I teach. What will they do one day? I see so much possibility. I can change the world, with just one child."

"It's crazy, but that's life. There's so much we don't know …. waiting to be known."

"Are you dating anyone these days?"

"No, I haven't found the right one yet." He said.

"I see. We're both older now. Maybe you aren't looking in the right places. There's a world in which we dream and the one that exists right now. Think about it. I have to go."

She stood up. He hugged her.

"Will I see you again?" he asked her.

"Whenever you want."

MOM AND DAD

Our lives began with you
Now there are four of us.
On this day we celebrate
The life you started
The love you shared
To make us whole.

It wasn't always easy
Making our way in a new country
Somehow we survived
Lost jobs and funerals
Heartbreak and fighting
Uncertainty and fear.

We were champions of our own belief
That we could achieve
With opportunity for all of us
As long as we tried.
Dad worked and mom took care
You were a great team.

From graduations to birthdays
And everything else
You worked side by side
To provide for us the best you could.
It was more than we needed.
Life has been a blessing
Because of you.
There's no way to repay you for that.

THE 4 GREAT TOWERS

Every man has an obligation to his family, however great or small, we honor them as we see. For some we provide, for some we protect. Everything that must be done. Beyond our own needs are the family, and how we serve them. Society too is before. On this road, we yield to what is peaceful and just.

Audrey had always sought to take care of his parents. He studied medicine for that reason. Suddenly a world opened that needed his help. He had a greater calling in the world, far beyond what he dreamed.

One day, on a day like today, he flew away. He didn't know where he was going. He let the wind take him. He soon landed in a place where the sun was dim, fading out. Half the town was in shade even in the day, as if something had eclipsed the earth. Audrey asked what was wrong. A woman replied that the sun was losing power, very soon the earth would be dark. If that happened, it would be difficult to survive. Food sources would die, their way of living would be gone. The gravity of the situation was hard to forget. The people were filled with anxiety. Everyone was trying to conserve light for the future, if it ever came. The last hope was the four great towers. They were lighthouses that stood at the four corners of the town. It was there the people had gathered as a way of adapting. The center of town was being deserted and yet so much of the commerce and culture was there. It was as if a ship had split in two and the people had run for safety at the corners. It wouldn't last long. Fairly soon they too would sink. These were the circumstances he found. If only there was a way to conserve the light from the four great towers, they could survive.

How long had it been like this? They said they didn't notice at first. The days were colder. They blamed it on the weather and the effects of the pollution on the sky. There was less and less daylight. It was as if a curse was set over the town, a plague of darkness. No one understood not even the great scientists who came from far away. The town looked to the men of faith, who said whatever it was, it was there for a reason. Audrey asked if there was anyone who had an answer. In the center of town was a healer, a wise man, who many took as a fool. He believed in various treatments and made remedies no one took. He believed in the great spirits of the earth, yet none would see him through. Many believe he had lost his mind. It was true he was old and very odd in certain ways. He was one of the few who decided not to leave, even when the sun was fading. He said it would return one day. He said it was up to them. Everything they needed they had. They had to restore the sun somehow with the light of the great towers. It was impossible they said. Another foolish idea. Maybe he was right Audrey said, "I'll hear what he has to say."

In the center of town was a sign, 'The Mystical Healer Reeza'. It was a small hut separate from the other stores. Audrey pushed the beads and walked in. Reeza was a short man with a large belly and a beautiful band on his head with feathers sticking out. He wore no shirt and only a small loin-cloth like a sumo wrestler. His face was painted white with two strips of red across the eyes.

"My name is Audrey." He said, "I heard about your ideas. About the 4 great towers and using their light to power the sun. How do we do it though?"

"There's a precise angle if all the lights were directed equally, someone could reflect it to the sun. We have to turn all the lights to the center of town, when the sun is weakest. How I don't know."

"I could use my umbrella. It allows me to fly. I think it's strong enough to bend the light. We'll have to try."

"Let me see it."

Reeza felt the weight of the umbrella and saw the mystical power it held. "I might be able to bless it somehow. Make it stronger. There's no greater power than the lights of the 4 towers and you need a way home when this is done."

"I trust you. Do what you have to do."

He took the umbrella and forged it in fire, adding some mystical powder that made the flames grow. A strong aroma took the room. Different colors filled the air.

"There's a mathematician named Lewis Gomen who resides by the first tower. He'll have to calculate the angle this has to be held, and exactly where to stand. He's a young man, quite brilliant. Tell him I sent you and see what he says. Give him this." He handed Audrey a small pouch with a string tied around it "You must move fast!"

Audrey bowed his head and parted. He asked the townspeople where tower one was located. They said it was southeast of here. A twenty minute walk. It was day but there was no light, only shade along the way. The further he moved to the corner of town there were more and more people and they were frightened and restless. There weren't enough lights for the school and there was nowhere to play. They were pushing and shoving, fighting for every inch of light. In a small apartment with a single bed, he met Lewis Gomen. He told him everything. "Will it work?" he asked him.

"Let me see the umbrella." Lewis said, "Wow. It's far stronger than I expected. If we find the right angle it could be the trick we needed." The tension in his face disappeared, he was almost gleeful. He went to work on his writing board that hung on the wall beside his bed. Several times he crossed things out and scratched his head. He stood back. "What am I doing wrong?" he asked himself. He worked like this with the one candle on his table lighting the board. Several hours went by. Audrey sat quietly. He tried to understand and helped him when he could. Some of it made sense, other parts were harder. He worked diligently. It was hard to tell the day from the night.

"This is it." He said, "The lights have to be directed this way at this time and you'll have to stand right here." His hand was shaking. He took the small pouch Audrey gave him and took some of the herbs and mixed it with water, and drank it down. He stopped shaking. His hunched appearance was gone, and he was firm and resolute. "The umbrella has to be held this way." He showed him. "It's not as complicated as I thought, but I had to make sure. I'm still not sure how much power the sun will need. That I leave to faith. If the lights are strong enough and directed with such force they burn right through you. I had to be careful. I'll follow you. I'll set the lights myself. It'll be hard to get in. I know the keeper in tower one. Convincing the others will be harder. I'll talk to him and see what I can do. Say nothing of Reeza. They won't listen to anything he says. We have to go now. We can't waste time. All the light in the sun will be gone in a matter of days."

GUIDING LIGHT

The sky was overcast. The time of final darkness was almost there. The people were mad. There was hysteria. The sun would come up again but without power how could they live? The police were out trying to maintain order. There were great fires all around. The animals too were wild. Every night it came like this. Faces stared out windows lit by candles, wondering when it would be safe again. It was in this general mood, Audrey and Lewis stepped out, Lewis leading the way. There was a crowd by the first tower. They had to fight their way to the front. People were knocking but the door was locked. "Go home." A voice said.

"We need more light!" the people shouted.

"This is the most I can give you right now." He replied. Lewis went up to knock.

"Jim it's me, Lewis. I have an idea. I need your help. Let us in for a minute. I'll explain." The door unlocked and the two of them went inside. The door locked again.

"This is madness Lewis. What is it you want?"

"I think we can restore the light to the sun. We need all the lights of the 4 towers directed at the center of town first thing in the morning. I made calculations. We need a certain angle for all the lights at a certain power, directed at the sun. Audrey here will help us. He has an umbrella strong enough to hold the force of the light. If we're not careful, we could destroy everything. The whole town will burn and the people die."

"They'll die anyway if the sun loses power. They may even kill each other." Replied Jim.

"I need you to call the keepers of the other towers. Instruct them what to do." Lewis pulled out a scroll that was blue with white ink where he wrote down the masterplan. Lewis explained everything carefully, simply, so he would understand. Jim had confidence in the plan. He knew the power of the lights in the 4 towers were stronger than anything the town had. They had to use it. He never shone it at the power they needed because it was a danger to the people. Now they had to throw caution to the wind. The other towers were far away. Jim made calls to all the keepers. He relayed the message. It was urgent. He too explained everything carefully, as far as he knew.

"We'll make our way to the center of town." Said Lewis, "It might take us some time. Remember, everything depends on us now. The people will be sleeping when the sun comes out. We'll be waiting. It's the only way to keep them from harm and save us all."

"I understand." Jim said, "I'll do exactly as you told and so will the other keepers. I assure you. Let's pray it all works out."

With this Lewis and Audrey went to the center of town. It was a further walk than Reeza's, for the center of town was large and he was on the outskirts. The true center of town was deeper.

"This is the spot." Said Lewis, "We wait here until the sun comes up. They'll set the lights at that time. This is the angle." He showed him. "I calculated everything including your height and where to direct the light in the sun so it consumes it faster without burning out the lights. There's a lot of factors here. I trust my work though. I checked everything a thousand times. There's still a risk to you."

"I understand and I'll do it." Audrey said.

"We've never done this before. Set the lights at that power. My father helped design the 4 towers. The keepers were sworn to never let the real power of the lights be known or ever used, unless a great emergency came. I'm one of the few who know. I too was sworn to secrecy."

They waited patiently, tired as they were from not sleeping at night. Audrey needed to save all his strength for the lights of the great towers. As the sun began to rise, Lewis could see the lights turning one by one. There was no one near, only a few stray people in the distance. First tower one, then tower two, the third, the fourth. They were all concentrated at one point, not yet strong, where Audrey was standing. Suddenly the sun fixed itself in one spot and all four lights of the great towers came at full force, charging at him like a cannonball at every direction. It was too much to hold. He sent the lights upward, deflecting them.

"Plant your feet." Lewis said, "Use all your strength!"

Audrey gently lowered the umbrella which had the power to hold the light. He fixed his elbow at the angle he was taught, and pushed forward pushing the lights, reflecting them back at the sun. Slowly he could see the sun glowing, as if it were fed.

"Push Audrey, push! Fight the light."

He used all the strength he had. He was being pushed back, the lights were strong. The people in town were waking up. They hadn't seen the sun like this for a long time. People stood outside their doors, staring at the sun. Audrey was fighting as best he could. His legs were suddenly tired. He was ready to give up. He looked at Lewis who was smiling.

"It's working Audrey. The sun is getting brighter. Stay in place."

Audrey concentrated all his strength. The umbrella was working in a way he never knew it could. It was all thanks to Reeza who was outside hopping with joy. Audrey stood there, unwavering. The sun restoring before their eyes like charging a battery. Lewis was calculating how far it had restored. Almost 80%.

"Keep going. You're almost there."

The people were dancing in the street. Hugging, embracing. Soon the sun was fully restored and Lewis signaled to the keepers to turn the lights out. Reeza joined them and Audrey fell to the ground. They picked him up at both sides.

Very soon the town heard about Reeza's idea and he was hailed for his wisdom. No longer a fool. Audrey was able to recover soon. The calculations Lewis made were correct and the three of them were honored in town. The papers wrote about the way they saved the town. Audrey was a hero. He asked for nothing in return. He was proud of what he did and said it was a reward in itself. To have the power to help people is the greatest joy. Audrey never planned to be there at that time, to help these people and yet somehow destiny had called him there. It's hard to know where we'll be at any given moment, yet we make the most of what we're given, and do the best we can with what we have right now. Life is a mystery, an eternal question, waking us with insight at every step. What direction it leads us ...... we never know.

REALLOCATIONVILLE

In love we are ever seeking a way to distinguish ourselves from those around us. Something in the way of honor or beauty will hand us the advantage we need to show our fitness if life is a game. We all see the world differently, and every man will do good above anything, yet there is some truth that we must fight, each on his own, to survive. So the details matter if we must sell ourselves like products in today's world and tomorrow. As we live we consume, so we are no different than others, only in the aspect of what we see, what we desire. To have freedom is to have a choice. Equality cannot be forced in everything we do. By the same token, we are asked to live gracefully for that is the way of peace.

One day Audrey flew to a place he'd never seen. It was a small town with a sign that read *Reallocationville - Where every prayer, wish, or dream desired, is reassigned.* He thought it very strange. The town was bright with low buildings and friendly people. They all wore similar clothes and drove similar cars. Even the houses were the same. They had all the same haircuts and even talked the same. It was hard to tell the difference between one person and the next. As he wandered he stepped into the immigration office. There was a window with a small man sitting in a chair, talking to people as they entered. Many people were waiting, filling out paperwork as they were seated. There was a line but it moved quickly. Everything was in order. Audrey spoke with the man at the counter for some time. Soon an argument ensued.

"If you live here you'll have to cut your hair."

"Not a chance."

"Yes .... And you can't wear such bright colors. It's not fair to the others."

"But they can wear bright colors?"

"Some of them. For the less appealing."

"You're kidding me?"

"No, I assure you I'm not. Everything here is about fairness. One cannot be too handsome."

"What about the girls?"

"The blonde ones have to wear ponytails. Some are not allowed to be blonde. It's not fair to the others. Some are blessed with too much. Distractions we call them."

"How do I stand out against the others?"

"Everyone here is the same."

"What about the tall men? It's not fair to me."

"They're not allowed to have good jobs. It's only fair."

"And the short men are?"

"Some of them. The less appealing."

"This is ridiculous."

"Only modesty."

"You can't regulate that."

"But we do …."

"Am I allowed to work out?"

"To a degree. One cannot be too muscular. It creates body envy. We don't want that here."

"So you want to enforce laziness?"

"There are merits to that. One cannot be too smart or too strong. We have to control the people somehow."

"So what do you suppose we do if we can't read or exercise?"

"There's television. Drama, sports, whatever you like."

"What about freedom of speech?

"There's no such thing. Freedom is a word that likes to bend. The people here keep their mouth shut. You watch what you say because we watch when you say it. We have eyes and ears everywhere, but don't let that scare you. Anywhere you go there's order. We go about it differently."

"Yes, I can see that. Are there jobs?"

"For the men, yes. The girls are taught to not do well in school. It's not fair to the boys who have to make a living."

"So the girls get bad grades on purpose?"

"They lower their standards, try a little less. This is the way the world works, at least here. Any other questions?"

"Yeah, how do I get out of here?"

"Follow this road a little further. Either North or South. Just beware there are rules anywhere you go.'

"I'm starting to get that...."

"Well, we wish you luck wherever you go, but we warn you, there's no place like here."

Audrey turned to the men behind him. "Why would anyone want to live here?" he asked.

"It sounds like hell ...." Said the first man as he stepped away.

"I'm pretty sure it is." Replied Audrey.

"For many, there's no other way. Choices are few. It's either live here or be homeless." Said the second man.

"There's always a choice. There's other places." Audrey reminded.

"Not with this quality of life."

"You have to be kidding me."

"We have a house, we have food. There are rules anywhere you go."

"Not like these. This is like prison .... for the will."

"It's not wise to question other people's choices. We all have conditions that brought us to this. So there are rules? So what? Some of us have more faults than you. You've been blessed with so much, a lot of that you deserve."

"I believe that if you work hard you should have a good life."

"It is a good life. There are limits though."

"Who's to say that?"

"I don't want to argue. This is our life."

"Are you happy?"

"Yes we are."

"Then I'll say no more."

So many systems of government. Do people give up something, for the hope of getting something like peace and security? If so, what do we give up and who says? Every man has a voice and a responsibility to use that voice for the greater good. What's the price of happiness? Only you can judge. Be active in all matters great and small that determine your well being. What's local today may be national tomorrow. Express your civic duty, or somebody else will, and you might not like it. Take advantage of what you have because people die for that. All these things I mean, consider them.

Audrey stepped out and walked away from town. There's a whole world out there waiting to be known, if we look beyond ourselves and the small part of the world we see. Different customs survive in many different lands, all for the safety of the people that live there. We all define a good life differently, and so it makes sense that there are varieties of joy, varieties of peace. One shared purpose can have many ways to bring it about. That's the beauty of life as shaped by the government we submit to. As we believe, they seek to uphold.

(SONOGRAM)[1]

You have lived without love for all these years. It will follow you down. This will be a habit too, unless you break it. Now there is a heartbeat, soft and still. Everything you need to know for life. We are born within, not to be without.

A gentle push, a new beginning. The tears that call for you. A mother, a father, a child. Never to be alone again.

This is joy. Truly. Having it, not chasing.

It was always assumed that Audrey would make a good marriage and settle down young, so when he didn't, it was a cause for concern. Many people had tried to play matchmaker and set him up with someone, which always frustrated him. The major decisions in his own life were decided by others, as if he didn't know what to do. It was true he was shy at times, but so many girls sought after him. He felt pressure from everyone. He was always busy, but now he had some time to look.

"It's a balance Audrey, there's never a right time. You'll always have something getting in the way. You have to make room for a relationship. It's about sacrifice. You have to give up some of your own free time. I know that's hard for you.

---

1   Title read silent.

If you don't look when you're young, you might see your life pass by and you'll still be alone. That's not to say you're too old, but you have to try. There's no perfect girl out there. It takes effort and investment. Find someone you're attracted to and you have common interests and views and ideals, and shape them into the person you want them to be. You have to be open. It takes compromise. You've always been independent, but as you get older you have to change. You don't want to wake up to an empty life, not when you're 50 years old. Having money or a career won't be enough. It might buy you happiness in the short term, nice food, vacations, cars. It won't last though. Those are temporary ways to stay happy. I know you always cared about mom and dad but you have to start your own life. Before Sadie I had no direction. Now I have a reason to live. It sounds silly, but you don't know how powerful love can be." Said his brother Diyon.

"I know you mean well D. It's just I worked so hard to get to this point. All that time I was studying, I was dreaming of the girl who would make it all worth while."

"You might have missed her though. There's so many girls I've seen you pass on. You're always so protected. Give them a chance. Someone."

"It's just whenever I do something I like to go all the way. I don't want to choose the wrong girl and be stuck with her. It sounds dumb, but I don't want to hurt anyone. I've seen so many couples that seem like they're happy, but they fight all the time or they ignore each other. I don't want to be like that. Choosing a partner is the only family you get to choose. It's so important to me, that I pick the right girl. I always had this vision of the family I want. I haven't met the one to give me that."

"At a certain point you have to choose one and go with it. People have layers you don't know, unless you give them a chance. I know you're smart and I trust your ability to know what's right, but you seem to analyze things without trying them. Maybe you were busy before. It's not easy what you do. Who knows, maybe it's all timing. You might wake up tomorrow and you'll see the girl you always wanted, right there, waiting. It might be the ghost of someone you knew in a new form, some feature you desired taking life, like re-incarnation. You might find something you missed in some-one you never knew, like they were meant for you. If you feel it, don't ignore it. Follow it. See where it takes you. Embrace love, how wonderful, how mysterious it can be. That's what I want for you."

"That's what I want for myself. That's all I really want. Trust me. I don't want to be alone. It feels like a curse. It's my own fault though. I chose to be this way."

"You have an anxiety disorder. It's not the same. It's not your fault."

"I think everyone's got something though."

"Trust me. It's not the same."

Just then, Sadie arrived. She hung the keys by the door.

"Hey Audrey. Did he tell you the news?"

"What news?"

"It's gonna be a girl!" she said beaming.

"Congratulations! Isn't that what you wanted?"

"Secretly yes." She laughed.

"I think it's great to know. Now you can plan everything ahead. You can decorate the baby's room. If you need any help let me know." He grabbed D's shoulder. "I'm so happy for both of you."

"You're gonna be an uncle." Said Diyon, "Are you ready for that?"

"I'm gonna spoil her." He laughed.

"I know you will." Said Diyon.

"How do you feel?" asked Audrey looking at Sadie.

"Excited. Nervous. This is our first child, it's always gonna be that way. I think we're ready though."

"Ready for anything?" he asked Diyon.

"I'm ready for anything." He smiled.

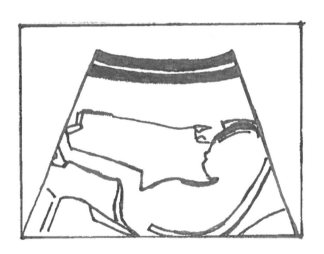

RESURRECTION DRUGS

What does it mean to save a human life? At what point are we doing more than God's work? To be a physician is to have great power and so we use it for the good of all, abiding by the laws and practices we were sworn to. New advances will always bring questions of what is ethical and what is right. These are questions not for the individual but for those who govern and set the standards for all medicine. It's no easy thing, when so much good and so much evil can be done.

After graduating Audrey decided to take some time off to figure things out. Most nights he stayed up late. He watched tv like he never did before, not for a long time. He wrote every day. He spoke with Teller on the phone and saw her every once in a while. Like old times. They were young when they met and still they had a place for each other. Warmer now. Deeper in affection. "I was alone for a long time, one day she was there." Audrey thought as he laid down to sleep.

He woke to the sound of the television, half sleeping. It was an advertisement for a new drug. *"If you could pay to bring your loved ones back, what would you pay?"* There was a man on tv with dark glasses, a bald head. He was self-possessed in a way Audrey couldn't pin down. There was something disturbing about him. "I've seen him before," he thought, "When I was in the clinic in New York. He was trying to sell the doctor the drug, but he wanted no part of it. He said it was highly unethical. The man said he was a fool. That it was a goldmine. That was years ago."

The man claimed he could resurrect the dead only for a short while. No one believed him. How was that possible? The phone calls were coming in fast. So many questions. He stood there patiently answering every question in scientific terms. "These wonder drugs can restore life, I assure you. The heart beats again, the function of the human brain revitalized, as if a day had not gone by. Even those long dead."

His name at the bottom was Dr. Volta. He went on to explain his training in the military, where the idea began. For years he tested the drug, working in the laboratory alongside a small team. They were highly gifted, desiring nothing but to share the drug with the world. The moment was now. It was the dawning of a new day. "The future is here" he claimed. Audrey couldn't believe it.

To prove their point they showed a clip in a morgue where a man had been dead for days. There was a man who claimed to be a forensic pathologist who confirmed the man was dead. He said it was impossible to restore life at this point. He had died from a hemorrhage in the brain. His body was cold and would soon decay. Dr. Volta injected him with something. In a matter of seconds the other doctor said there was a pulse. Very faint.

"My God! What is that? What's happening?" There was breathing. The chest went up and down. There was a violent jerk, a terrible cough, and suddenly the eyes opened. The other doctor backed away. "In all my years …."

There was a grin on Dr. Volta's face, then his eyes turned sharply and looked at the screen. "This is just the beginning … " He placed his hand over the body as if calming a child. Whatever bleeding had occurred inside the brain was healed and a force of life returned, limb by limb. Slowly, gently. The toes, the knee, the arm. More coughing, as if choking. Then a voice, "Where am I?"

"What do we do now? This is a miracle. He's alive. He's really alive! What did you inject him with?" said the doctor now horrified.

"Resurrection drugs. We have the power. Think of all we can do now? First attend to the body." They both held the body before it rolled to the ground. "You're alive again. Isn't it wonderful?"

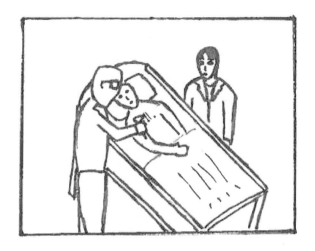

Audrey stared at the screen as if it were a joke of some kind. There was nothing funny about it. This was a set up he thought to himself. It wasn't real. There was nothing in the medicine he studied that made it make sense. He looked at every possibility. If the man was truly dead, brain dead, how could it be? A hoax he said. Nothing more. This will all just disappear in a few days. Some crazy sensation to fool people, get money somehow. Why would they do that though? Why experiment like this? "I have a feeling something terrible will come" Audrey said, "If it's true, worse than anything we've seen."

MIRACLE MAN

Everything was poorly planned,
The sinner saved and mother damned.

Audrey woke the next morning doing all the research he could. Who was Dr. Volta? He was highly educated, holding chairs at UPENN and Johns Hopkins Medical School where he was let go for some kind of altercation. He had published papers on his research going back 30 years. Audrey read through them. He didn't understand the dynamics of the drug, how it worked in the body. What did it do? Was it safe? It was frontline news on every paper. You couldn't turn on the tv without hearing about it. Stocks for the drug had soared. He was making millions of dollars in a matter of days. There wasn't a person that hadn't lost someone they wanted to see again. What the drug promised was something no one had ever dreamed before. Was he able to control the bodies? How long would they live? So many questions to find out. Audrey picked up the phone to call Teller.

"Did you see the news?"

"Of course. Are they real?"

"I'm not sure. We have to do something."

'What's he after, money? Power?"

"I have no idea. He's a hero, a genius, that's what they're saying."

"I don't buy it."

"He was selling the drug years ago. I saw him in person. He was guarded, like he was hiding something, No one took him seriously. He was angry, driven by that. Sometimes the most brilliant men are the ones we fear the most. Right now he's playing God and it's dangerous."

Teller was trying to dig a little further.

"I'm reading something right now. He's from a long line of physicians. He inherited money from his father and built his own laboratory Fabian. It's not far from here. We'll drive there tonight and see if we find anything."

The two set off that night dressed in black. Audrey slipped on gloves. "Wear these." He said as he handed her a pair.

"I have binoculars. We'll see how they close at night. It's not gonna be easy to get in."

One night soon became three as they watched from a distance. As they assumed, the building was heavily guarded with surveillance. "Do you know anyone who could get us in?" Audrey asked.

"I have a friend. We'll have to find out who works there. Use their phones to bug them. It's gonna take some time."

They plotted carefully. Teller's friend Jason was a master surveillance expert trained with the Navy Seals. He had retired early after selling shares of the technology he developed. He didn't trust Dr. Volta either and was glad to help any way he could. Three men stepped out every day for lunch. Jason was able to follow them one day. When one of them took out their phone, Jason was able to slip a tracking device. From there he could hack into the phone and gain access to the surveillance system. He had all the information he wanted. He could now safely enter the passcodes that were scanned on the phone. Using the phone's camera he was able to make out the groundwork of the building, little by little. Every step he took he saw more of what they needed. He was able to capture conversations between the coworkers, mostly business.

"He's not only raising the dead but controlling their minds as well. It isn't for the good of the people but for himself. He's secretly plotting to build an army with all the bodies recovered. He hasn't figured out how to preserve the people he brings to life. They eventually die again. He's using the money to fund his research. No one else would support him. That's what the fight at Johns Hopkins was about. He bypassed the standards and practices knowing the drug would sell. It hasn't been approved by the FDA. It never would be." Reported Jason a few days later.

"I think we have everything we need." Said Audrey.

"We need proof though." Said Teller.

"We have all his communications. All we have to do is reproduce them in court. They'll have to forfeit the information." Said Jason.

"You make it sound so easy." Said Teller.

"They'll be a bounty on our heads for sure." Said Audrey.

"I'm willing to risk that."

"So am I." said Jason.

"We'll have to use the media." Audrey mentioned, "Whatever's happening in there; it can't be good."

Far away in the city, Dr. Volta was administering the drug for those in need, feeding the deepest desires of people; fathers with lost daughters, children and their parents, the ones who died alone, never saying goodbye. A last chance for all of them. "If you can bring my mother to life, I'll give you anything." Said a young man. The bodies were delivered one by one to those in line. Dr. Volta uncovered the body, "I'll do as you said. How long she stays I don't know."

"Even a few minutes would be enough." He said, "Thank you so much." They waited together. Dr. Volta took her arm and injected the drug at once. Only a few seconds went by.

"What's happening?" she said "What is this!?"

"Mom…." He cried, "It's me Bill, your son. Do you remember?"

"Bill, what's going on? I'm scared. Why am I here? Where are my clothes!?" He grabbed her hand as she covered herself.

"Don't be scared. I'm here. We're at a clinic. I thought we lost you," he was sobbing, "You're here again. I love you. Please mom. I love you. No matter what remember that.

I love you." She sat up wrapping the sheet around her. He hugged for a long time. "All I wanted was to tell you that."

"I love you too Bill, I'm cold. I'm hungry."

He started crying. He hugged her again.

"We'll get you something, I promise. Just don't go away. Stay here with me. Mom. Please don't go away."

"I won't."

Dr. Volta stood there grinning. All those years of ridicule and suddenly everything was working.

"This is only temporary Bill." He reminded.

"Keep her here somehow. Please. Anything you can do. Just keep her alive. I'm not gonna lose you mom. Not again."

"She won't be here long Bill. Enjoy it while you can."

Her voice was failing. She fell back on the table.

"I think I'm gonna die Bill!" She was gasping for air. Almost convulsing. "Oh god!" Her arms grew stiff. Her eyes closed and she was gone.

"Mom!" he cried uncontrollably. "Thank you Dr. Volta. Whatever you want I'll pay you."

"You'll have a chance to do that. Take some time for yourself. I know it's hard to deal with. Sit down."

"Did that just happen?" He looked up at him. "Was that real? It's a miracle. What you did is a miracle."

"I wouldn't call it that." He said, "It's purely science."

He grabbed the doctor's hand with both of his and shook it profusely.

"Thank you for what you did. Thank you. Thank you. Thank you. That was a miracle, whatever you say …. that was a miracle …"

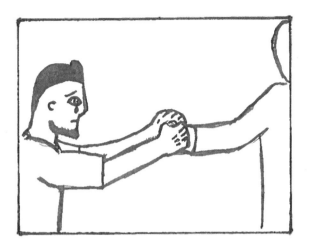

RESOLUTION

"What are your intentions, Dr. Volta, with these drugs?" asked a journalist. There was a crowd outside the clinic. Photographs were taken nonstop. It seemed like every major paper was there, every tv station. The line for the clinic was endless, with every new customer satisfied.

"I want to give the people what they want. Everything I ever wanted. To see the ones they love one more time."

"Isn't it dangerous?" said another voice from the distance.

"These men and women are dead already. Some longer than others. What I do is give them life. Isn't that what we do in medicine? Save people?"

"Isn't it too much power? What if people exploit this?"

"There's a great deal of power, you're right. It appears that medicine has always been that way. We work for the interest of the people we serve."

"Why are you charging so much?"

"These drugs have been heavily researched. We have to make up the costs for all the labor involved. The scientists who worked long nights to make this happen."

"Who's profiting the most. Isn't it you?"

"It's the people who gain the most. To see their loved ones again. With that, I must get back to work." The journalists turned to the people who were leaving the clinic. They asked them for their feedback. There was a great commotion as the bodies were lined up. There were caskets and stretchers, hospital beds rolling down the street. The cars were backed up. Everyone waiting for something that seemed like hope.

Later that day Audrey, Jason, and Teller were following the plans of Fabian. They had the inner workings of the company in their hands:

"We're moving on to phase 3. Tonight we test the drugs in the field. There's a higher dosage with a synergistic mind controlling effect. If we want absolute power, we have to be safe. We need an army and it begins tonight. You know where I'll be." Said the man on the phone.

They used the tracking device to find the precise location they were meeting. It was late at night 1 AM. They were in the graveyard in a small town digging out bodies by a white church. There were five of them. Three of the big men doing the physical labor, the two scientists waiting with their arms crossed. The scientists dressed in button down shirts with overcoats were quite anxious. "We need the bodies out quickly. There's not a lot of time to waste."

One of them paced between the tombstones muttering something, the other one checking his phone. Soon the bodies were lifted up from where they were. Four coffins of the recently deceased laid aside. It was time for the scientists to do their work. The four bodies were sat up with two in a row. They injected the medicine. Violent fits began and soon they were calm. A hand raised against the side of the coffin, a knee lifted up. "Do not be alarmed." The taller scientist said, "You are under control. Follow my voice and do as I say."

"Rise up and come out." Said the other.

Audrey and his friends watched in horror. The bodies did exactly as they were told.

"I've seen enough, let's call the police." Audrey said.

"I called them as soon as we got here." Said Jason.

"All of you freeze!"

Suddenly four headlights turned on. There were flashlights all around. The police had them cornered. "Keep your hands up!"

One of the scientists reached in his coat for a gun and he was shot in the arm. The four bodies stood there confused.

"Do something! Get them!" the taller one shouted.

The dead bodies went after the cops and shots rang out. One of the heads was knocked clear off.

"What the hell is this!?" said the first cop.

"How do we kill them? Be careful." Another one said.

Meanwhile the two scientists were handcuffed with the other three men. The resurrected bodies were shot to the ground.

"This is crazy." One of the cops said as he stood over the body.

The five men were placed in the cars and taken off.

"Our job here is done." Said Teller.

"I hope so ….. but I don't know." Said Audrey.

The next morning Fabian was again front page news, but for a different reason. Conspiracy charges were brought against Dr. Volta and all the men who worked for him. His clinic was shut down along with the laboratory and all its operations. People were shocked. What seemed like a good thing for many had turned into one of the greatest tragedies the nation had seen. It's always best to keep on guard when things that seem too good to be true, are shown to be false and hope that felt so near is suddenly taken. Dr. Volta had many ideas, some of them with a true basis to help people, yet in his quest he had forgotten why he started. The desire to rule and assert his power, consumed his mind like a sickness. His great advancements would one day help a great many, yet for him it was never enough. Everlasting glory, an everlasting name, those were the things he wanted, for any price.

THE BUILDING

In the fall of that year, Audrey found a new place to live. It was a beautiful complex a few towns over from his parents. At first everything seemed to be going well. His parents helped him furnish the place. He had everything he needed. He settled into a domestic way of life. He cooked and cleaned and lived very quietly. Every day he wrote something and posted it for all his friends to see. It was a sort of research on a way of life he never knew. For years he studied medicine and nothing else. He lost touch with people and why he worked so hard for all those years. Wasn't it a family he always wanted? Now he was taking the steps to build that life and it started with his apartment.

Every day he visited the coffee shop for a cup of tea, sometimes two. He sat there reading, some days writing. As he sat there one day, he felt there was someone watching him. He let it slip his mind. The next day he noticed the same thing. This time it was someone different eyeing him from a distance. When Audrey turned his head, he pretended not to be staring. "Why would anybody be watching me?" he thought. When he went back to his home, there were others like the people in the coffee shop, moving here and there as if they were acting. Everything staged from the moment he walked inside. Who were these people and what did they want? When he introduced himself the names they gave all seemed to be false. When he went to the coffee shop he felt everything was rehearsed as if he were a spectator. He had always seen life as a movie, now it seemed like suddenly it were. Even the people behind the counter were studying his every move and reacting. He felt uncomfortable. Every time he gasped for air they suddenly shifted as if to irritate him and then observe. "Why are they doing this?" he wondered. He wasn't harming anyone. He was just drinking tea.

When he went back to his building he noticed it had an eerie resemblance to the home he grew up in. He stuffed his hands inside his pockets and lowered his head as he walked in.

"How are you?" said the woman inside.

"I'm fine. It's been a strange day."

"Aren't they all?"

His eyebrows knitted closely as he looked down avoiding eye contact. He pushed the button for the elevator. "Hurry up" he thought. There were two people waiting, every look rehearsed. What do they expect me to do? He stood in between them and rushed out when they arrived at his floor. What is this place? Audrey found his keys and turned the door. He locked it quickly. "Either I'm going crazy or there's something more to this than I thought."

He had gone from studying medicine to being the object of study. Every breath he took they interpreted the meaning. Every window in the building was gazing out at him and he didn't know who was looking. He wasn't safe even in his room. He closed the blinds but they wouldn't close all the way. As he turned them he grew more and more frustrated. Even the rumble of the cars outside had some kind of meaning, a counterpoint to every thought he had. Motioning as he did, making noise with him. The whole building and the city itself was now a part of him. The next day as he stepped out he saw his youth reflected in the children in the building, fragments of himself. The beautiful ladies that passed by him, were women he had known so many years ago. All of this went on for some time.

One day his mother called to tell him a distant relative had moved into the building. Of all the buildings, why this one? He went to see him and when he did a flood of memories came back. He couldn't let go of the past, it was always there. Even the scents that lingered in the building, reminded him of something, along with the sounds that followed him wherever he went. Everything a sign. The litter, the mail, the walkways, the steps, the one stone upturned were all a trigger for some thought. All of it some kind of data for something. Classified information to someone. Every action and reaction.

WHAT IS RESEARCH?

What are the methods we use to gather information? Who's to collect and who's to control? What are the repercussions? How do we avoid hurting someone? We go to great lengths for order, yet how far is too far?

Audrey found himself the prisoner of research. Why he didn't know. Everything he learned taken for granted. It was hard to fight so great a force. Everywhere he turned there were lies, deceit, so much denial. He was helpless like a child. As the time went, he slowly became one. All his years of learning were suddenly gone. Everything he built taken. All he had was the apartment he lived in and the voice he had. "What do I do now?' he thought, 'How do I end this?" It was a nightmare.

All his books were taken and replaced with nonsense, reproductions, fake writing. In the land of the free he had no freedom. No one believed him. There was no proof they said, but every day was proof for him, however hard to discern for others. In the slightest things he felt disgraced, his education set back, his career. It was all taken. He was left with only shame and fear. Every morning when he woke he felt he had no reason. "What a sad existence." He thought to himself, "Why me?" The lines between living and dreaming were blurred. So much pain, and yet he bore it like some great sufferer. He had felt this before. This grave injustice though was something new. He had always had freedom. Now he longed to have it back. His old life. To have a wife and children was all he wanted. What was he up against? There was no way to know. "Will it ever end?" he said to himself. Days became weeks, and weeks years. Every day he grew older and had nothing to show for it, just an empty apartment and an empty life. Why? "What is this madness?" he asked. He was given only vague answers, large things to assume. It's hard to see the end of something, standing in the middle. "I will not fight this," he said, "I will surrender." Somehow he hoped it would bring him freedom.

He lived in a world of actors. There was no truth. "This is not the way I wanted things to be." He said. He had always been a long term person, now he only saw the end of the day and the start of a new one. There was no way further. Everyone he came across was paid to be there; part of the protocol. Much of the time he thought it was his mental health they were questioning. He was of sound mind though, as sharp as he ever was. He hardened himself with exercise knowing it would strengthen him mentally and physically. It was true he could eat whatever he wanted and go wherever he pleased, yet there were no bounds to the grand deception he was under. However far he went they'd follow him. From an outside view it was a normal life, inside it was a cruel punishment falsely made yet purposely directed. As with the greatest human crimes, the reasoning was doubtful, faith misguided. There was no just reason for this. It was all in bad taste.

However some may gain by the plans we lay, it should not come from the willful pain of others, not as he suffered. He would never have these years again, kept from the very things he wanted, that he deserved. So he wrote each day to send the message he was still there, in sound mind, waiting to be saved by the God he prayed each night. Even his bible, all his holy books, were taken. There was no refuge except the one he had inside himself. So he clung to this light, waiting for good news to come as he always saw it would somewhere inside. "I will not be broken." He said, "I will overcome. Every day is a challenge, but I will face it bravely. That is the way my father taught me and I will not forget. Wherever they take me, I will endure. Anything and everything for the sake of the family. The one I have and the one I know will be."

FALLING DOWN

Soon Audrey learned that the research he had started as a grad student had somehow followed him. They were using his own ideas and applying it to him. His study on serotonin and the cause of anxiety. He had a great fascination with how the brain worked. It was the reason he studied medicine, at least initially. There was a whole world to be discovered. The building he was in, was his own mind. Every room a story of his past and the people he knew. Someone else had created it. It was an experiment testing the drugs he was taking. These were clinical trials. They had been going on for years. Research and development for a brighter future, free of anxiety. It was true that millions of people were suffering each day. Now they had the drugs to cure them. They weren't used as broadly as they could be. Now they were seeing what they could do. It was no excuse to treat someone the way he had been treated. For four years he was tortured, years before tested. They were using him for everything he had. Audrey didn't mind helping, but they had gone too far. His private life made public to push him for the safety of the drugs and what they allow.

Audrey lived as a prisoner waiting each day to be released, as if it were a dream to put away, cast aside, and never go back. He had a feeling he was helping someone, but the question of time and the many others before him, never went away. He didn't know that the funding for the research was fading out. The research was almost complete. Even still, the media outlets were showing false news everyday that he learned to ignore completely. He didn't know what was going on in the world. He didn't know who was the president, only a false figure on tv. It was hard to believe it was America he was living in, but that's the power of government if it's led astray. The people closest to him acted as if nothing were wrong. It was business as usual. Audrey wouldn't live that way. He knew this wasn't normal. It was as if someone were challenging his mental integrity, using his anxiety as a weapon against him. Whatever reasons they had were still unclear. The powers against him were so large, so organized, that he was unable to fight them. There was no one to place the blame, for the forces were always hidden. He was fighting with shadows. If he told his friends they'd think he was crazy. Some of them already did. They thought he had relapsed from his prior anxiety. It was a nervous ailment they said.

Who was the head of operations at this building? He had to know. One day he went to visit. It was an old lady in a pink blouse with pearls around her neck. The office was empty, most of the lights turned out.

"Who's behind this!?" he asked.

"Behind what? I don't know what you mean."

"Who's playing this game? Who's making a joke out of my life!?"

"I'm sorry you're upset, but I really don't follow."

"I'm not leaving until you tell me!"

"Please, calm down," she said, "I'll have to call the police if you don't.

The powers against him had the police on their side, if he fought them he'd lose. At this point, he didn't care.

"I'm not leaving until you give me some answers. I want my life back. Who's doing this to me? Why? When is it going to be over?"

He kept repeating the same questions and she was very concerned.

Finally she said, "I'm calling the police."

He sat in the corner of the room on the floor with his arms crossed. He wasn't leaving. He wanted answers. Soon the police arrived.

"Tell me what's going on? Who's playing this game!? I can't take it anymore."

The policeman grabbed his arm and he resisted. He finally tackled Audrey to the ground and handcuffed him. He led him outside where the Emergency Medical Services were waiting. They placed him on a stretcher in the back of an ambulance and he was taken away.

"I don't believe this." He said as he watched from the window as if he were moving in reverse. He was a doctor, now he was a patient again. He knew he wasn't sick though. There was nothing he could do. When they arrived at the clinic he was asked many questions. What medications he was taking. Did he have any contacts. He answered everything patiently, subdued by the whole treatment.

"I just want to go home." He said. It was too late now.

He was admitted for inpatient therapy. It lasted four weeks. He had a daily routine with meals and activities. His clothes were brought one day. He was under constant observation, but he was used to that by now. The answers he wanted were never given. Someone was collecting data, somewhere out there he couldn't define. He made friends with the people around him. They were comrades under the same supervision for different reasons.

"Any place you go is about the people you're with and what you make of it." Told once said. He never imagined it would be in a place like this. As much as he hated to admit it, he grew used to the place. There was a comfort there, in being taken care of. He earned more privileges the longer he stayed. The right to shave, the right to use the gym, to leave the unit for a while. Slowly he felt better. He received therapy sessions, mostly group and some individual. He almost felt like he was wrong about everything. Was it just a nervous ailment? Then he reminded himself of everything that happened the last few years. There was far too much coincidence for him to ignore. This was a set up. More research. If he wanted to get out, he couldn't admit so. In time he was visited by his parents, he was given meetings with them. They looked concerned. What happened to their boy? Audrey knew he was on to something. He was let go after some time. He felt somewhat healed. Still it wasn't enough. When he got back to his old life, things would be the same.

He was fighting a system, a whole team of operations. He resisted peacefully as he had once learned. All the time knowing that there were people watching him. A thought occurred to him that they were guardians of some sort, protecting the city as they collected what they wanted. Always more information. Slowly with time Audrey moved with the current of what they were doing. He accepted there was nothing he could do. He had fought against the powers that be, and he had lost.

In a government of so much power there's not a lot to do, if you become the object of fascination and study as Audrey was. You can use every right you have and it may not be enough. He tried to surrender, to give himself up. Still the life he knew was gone. It wasn't until years later when every phase of the trials were complete, that Audrey was vindicated. Everything he thought was admitted and he was honored for his service to the country. He would be hailed as a hero. The anxiety medications they were testing would save millions. They were preventive medication that could stop everything from cancer to heart disease. Things as basic as hypertension and gastrointestinal troubles. It was a wonder drug. A breakthrough in medicine. It was not in vain, what he had studied and what he had learned, all his efforts to help people. In between that time he carried on as best he could, accepting the limits he was under. The family he so desired, would have to wait.

PART II

REASSEMBLE (IN THE NIGHT)

*There's a boy who walks in orange sandals on
his tiny brown feet, he's on a line for school with
the other children, when they walk, all my eyes
can see, are the orange sandals on his brown feet.
The introverted extrovert, he is no ordinary child,
he is the star of the moon unbowed, he is listening.*

"Sometimes I think about the things my parents did and it amazes me. How far they came." Audrey thought one day. He thought about the beautiful house he lived in, all the things he had, all the places he'd seen. None of this would be possible if his parents never boarded that flight to America, years and years ago. They were lucky and fortunate to be helped along the way, yet his father succeeded very much on his own merit and hard work. He had laid the foundation for everything Audrey stood on. Now he wanted to go back and see where his parents came from. He had been there twice before and every time it was different. He hadn't seen his family in so long. He wanted to see his grandma before she passed away. Something told him she didn't have long. She had lived a full life, sometimes lonely, somedays empty of meaning. "There's nothing left for me to do." she said one day. She had made peace with herself. "It's gonna be hard for mom to say goodbye." He thought. Her presence had been central to the family, holding everything together. She was the last of a generation that was slowly passing. The house she lived in, was the one his mother grew up, where everyone gathered with new husbands and children. She was that place. Her husband had died when she was young, leaving a family to care for. She had suffered and she had lived for them; a token of the past they never wanted to lose, for with her the past was alive.

Years ago Audrey had laid beside her in bed, when she was a guest there. She had traveled across the globe to see his graduation from the university. His mother was packing her things to leave. Audrey was just laying there on his side as she rested. He had fought with his mother while she was there. He had been studying so hard for exams. Now there was peace between them. She had slept alone for how many years. Now she felt she had someone. Audrey had never known her well. For a moment he saw the warmth and comfort she gave, as if he had known her far longer. To speak without speaking. Those were the things she understood. How she loved him, and he loved her. The child she knew, now a man, but still a child to her. She, the very likeness of his mother, in spirit and shape, connected in that moment forever to keep. They were three generations on a single bed, holding each other.

"I have to see her before it's too late. All of them. I miss them." Audrey thought about his little cousins, how they were all grown now, some of them married with kids. He was so busy for so many years, he hadn't had the chance to see them. Last time they met they had the best time. Audrey would never forget that trip, which was humbling and sweet and full of love both ways. Some things leave a mark on your life, and you always trace it back and forth in your mind as if it were a circle, that would play again everything you felt the first time. So many times alone he thought of them. He would hear music and oftentimes the words were written for him, or so he felt, the way they woke something deep inside, stirring all the feelings he had, the very thing that makes us human. It was that feeling he sought all his life, that made everything worth living. So in love with them and everything they symbolized, he had to go back. He wondered to himself, "Will it be the same?" and yet he knew that to see them and hear them would reverse every doubt he had inside and only add to what they had before. Soon the memories would fill him like his grandmother, so that the slightest touch would wake either joy or pain, as the nod of a head or weight of a step may do. That is what it means to grow old, and feel so much as if you cannot bear it, you are taken off your feet to sob. It's a gift and a curse to be old, so overwhelming it seems, that we are programmed to forget, the closer we near the end. We look forward to a new start somewhere far away, where the burden of living is somehow lighter and we are joined once more with all we hoped to see. Audrey felt that too. Going back home to where his grandma lived, was to trace that circle in his mind, and start again. That was all he wanted right now. It was only a means to get there that held him back. "There has to be a way" he thought.

One day his mother said, "We'll go together. You deserve it."

SEMINAL NOCTURNAL

The island you were born has known great suffering. That is the way it should be, for with it comes recognition of our differences and how we are the same. The appearance of things is not what they are. It is the true nature we seek to find. Where there is certainty there is peace, for there is no reason to fight when all are fed and dressed and spoken well with choice and free will. To work together is to be a greater force, for strength lies in numbers and this can only happen if we listen. That is the beginning, a nation reborn, to rise again. The world in a teacup. We take the shape of what we see, what we are taught to be. There is brilliance in the youth today, paving the way for tomorrow. The mistakes we made will stay in the past and *as we learn from them, we will not repeat them. We will love each other because that is the way forward.*

No man shall fall, as every man will work to keep each other standing.

We are one nation, not two. We will not be separated. There is no pain that we will not feel. Most of all we will try to understand that we all want the same things in life. If each man does his part we will succeed in new ways. Everything is waiting. The future is ahead. We are brothers and sisters. Tonight and ever so. No one will be left behind. There is much to gain, if we only try. That is what I hope tonight.

From the mask of so many ideas
 your eyes have spoken
to place the jewels of the sea,
Home at last.

ISLAND IN THE SUN

As soon as they arrived, his uncle opened the gate. He was waiting eagerly. He saw the car stop outside. That was the signal to let them in. The car pulled forward and Audrey stepped out with his mother and father. He kissed his uncle on both sides of the cheek, a typical greeting. He spoke the few words he knew and said, "How are you?" His uncle smiled and said he was glad to see him. 17 years. That was the last time they met. Audrey had completed his degree, and yet he felt the same, he was still a boy to them. His grandma was waiting, near the inside gate that was used as a door. From the gate you could see the front patio as the white bars had open spaces and everything was visible. The air and sunlight filtered in. When she saw him she kissed him. His parents came behind. His mother kissed her mom. This was as much for her as it was for him. They had stopped by 4 years earlier. Audrey was busy then. His mother told her about the flight, how they slept on the plane. It was a long flight nearly 20 hours. Audrey met a young woman on the way there. She was seated to his right. They struck up a conversation about literature and poetry, as they were both reading. It was a good way to pass the time, though his stomach was acting out making the ride less enjoyable. He tried to focus on what he was doing, reading or talking. She said that she had read books from around the world, and yet her favorite were the British writers. Audrey said he had always loved the French authors, though in general he agreed.

"I like the style of the French, but the output of England is so hard to compare. How many great poets from Shakespeare to Wordsworth and Tennyson. Then there's Dickens, Austen, Eliot, and Fielding too. That's just scratching the surface. I'll always have a special place for <u>Tom Jones</u> and <u>David Copperfield</u>." Audrey said, "I'll never forget them. I feel the same about the French though, Flaubert and Proust, Balzac and Montaigne. What incredible writers. <u>Madame Bovary</u> made me fall in love with reading again, when I was in college. It's not always the healthiest thing they talk about. Still the feeling, the manner they write, how it hits you, it's so profound. It's everything to me."

Soon Audrey was sitting in his grandma's looking out at the patio. "Everything looks the same." He thought, "It feels like home." It was late now, almost dinnertime.

"You must be hungry." His grandma said. She didn't know English and always spoke in the language they spoke there. Audrey could understand most of the things that were said, and like a young child searching for words, he spoke in little phrases he picked up here and there. This was always to the delight of his grandma, so he always tried. The best way to learn a new language is to practice in a native land. Hearing it so often, it's hard not to learn, like diving off the deep end and forcing yourself to swim when you don't know how. It wasn't all that scary though, having his family to guide him. Walking on the red tile floor, near the family room, the table was set and under the big fan that was always on, laid a feast of rice and fish and lentils and coconut and other exotic dishes. To give a good meal, was her way of showing how much she cared for them, saying welcome. All they had to do was eat. The more he ate, the happier she'd be. He was hungry by then. He served a little bit from each dish and kept going back for more. It wasn't every day he saw his grandma and had a meal like this. He was truly grateful for all they did. They were joined by his cousin and aunt and spoke freely. There was always dessert too. Audrey ate far too much in the end, but it was a day to celebrate. His cousin, now grown, sitting beside him. His grandma at the head of the table. She was weaker now. Most of the time she was in bed. Even sitting up was hard, but she had waited for them and she was glad. They went to the living room and talked, while Audrey's mother helped her get back in bed. Audrey and his cousin walked to the family room and sat down. All the memories came back, when he was here with his brother and they were still young. He thought of all the pictures when he was a baby. They were the same couches that the family shared for years. He looked up at the high ceiling and then at the picture of his grandfather in the corner table, who'd built this place. He was a very successful business person who made an empire selling auto parts to people. He had succeeded by his own labor and his talent with men. He never had much of an education his mother said. Still, with order and discipline and many years of hard work, he was able to rise in the country to a certain level of fame. He owned many properties and provided a great life for his children. He died when his mother was 14, and the family had to pick up where he left off. It wasn't easy. It was a shock to them and they did the best they could. Her brothers ran the business from what they knew. They suffered greatly. It was for this reason they were so close. They had to be. A perfect life may disappear without notice. That's what they learned from their father's death. It was for that reason Audrey's mother was overcome with fear throughout his life, always worried for Audrey and his brother, their health. It was why she esteemed doctors so highly in his eyes.

Now there was only his cousin before him and his father and uncle. Audrey asked his cousin about work and life and love. He said he was going to be married very soon and he showed him a picture of the girl. She was beautiful. He met her through friends. He said that work was busy as an accountant, that he had traveled recently for the job and it was fun. Audrey was happy to see the way he turned out. He said a few words to his aunt. She said she missed her other son who was far away. Audrey thought of his friends who he hadn't seen for a long time. It's funny the way that time separates us from all things, people move apart and yet the bonds we make remain. There was a girl Audrey knew once and he had known her only briefly, and yet he thought about her every day for many years. He touched her hand and she touched him back and he always wondered if that was the girl that God had meant for him. He looked again at his grandfather and the faces he hadn't seen for years. For now he was tired and his mother had come back. They said goodbye and left. It was a beautiful feeling to see these things.

The last time they were on the island they climbed a huge fortress made of rock. It was a long way up. His brother was there and he had filmed the whole thing. It was a natural scene, a real wonder for a small country like theirs. They saw the site from below, slowly they took steps and moved upward. Standing at the top, they looked around every which way. To be there beside his family and the journey there had to be symbolic in some way of where they had come from and how much they had achieved. He was proud of how loyal they had been. They were joined by many. It was as much a success for them as it was for him. Some things you never forget. He would return some other day. So many would follow.

The next morning when they woke they took a van and drove through the countryside. They took in the country for what it was and all it had become. It was modern with new roads and highways and beautiful temples along the way. Everywhere the culture could be felt in the shacks that sold food and other goods and the billboards that advertised local products with so many island girls that caught his eye. They drove up-country to where the tea estates were. Audrey sat beside his mother, the air condition on.

"I can't wait to see the rest of the family. Last time I was here they were children, and now some of them have children. I feel like my own life is going nowhere and it's sad. I'm happy for them though. It's just I feel I'm missing something. I'll complain another day. There's so much to be grateful, to be here now." He said.

"Enjoy the trip. Worry later." She laughed.

He looked outside the window and took it in. Their first stop was a beautiful lake. They walked around by the colorful flowers and the people who all looked like him. It was so different than America, with all the variety. There was a comfort and awareness that he was home, in the land of his people where he was born. A sense of belonging, of time and place, struck him in the most wonderful way as if he could breathe for the first time. There was no need to feel different, even without his parents, he was another part of the chain that bound him to the history of a land he was proud of. To outsiders he might look different in his western clothes, but when he breathed, really breathed the air, he was the same. He was five years old his nose had been unclogged after a long winter cold and the air was new to him and exciting. Just living was more than he could take and the power of his senses and how to grapple with them and tame them so he could be of use, was all that mattered then.

Audrey's father paid a small fee and they stepped into a boat. It was a calm ride. Audrey was so busy taking pictures, trying to get the right one, he almost lost the joy of the moment. He put his phone away and looked out. They had been on a boat when he was eight, the first time they were back on the island, and the floor of the boat had a clear panel where you could see all the life in the sea. He'd always remember that. Now he looked out at the lake and his mother and father, saying "This is peace." The boat returned to the dock and someone helped them out. Audrey's father tipped the boatman and they stopped by and had tea at a nearby shack. To be surrounded by all of them was like a giant family, so warm and dear to him. To feel connected that way, without speaking, on such a massive scale of a whole nation, was powerful and real. When he met his family later it would only cement that feeling, that he was meant to be here.

Soon they were back on the van. They had to take a narrow way that winded all around and made them dizzy. There was only room for one car so when another one came the other way, they had to back up and let them pass using whatever piece of land was there to stop. They traveled this way for 2 hours. Looking out the window, you could see how far up you were. It was a dangerous place to drive. There were edges and cliffs that ran all the way down, steeply. Audrey was afraid of heights, but he knew the driver was good and they would get there safely.

"How much further is it?" he asked Chamara.

"We're almost there." He said.

In a few minutes they pulled up to a tea factory that had been converted to a hotel. Chamara took out the bags and the hotel staff assisted him. They went to check in. Another member of the staff welcomed them with a hot towel and some tea. They drank up. They were in the van for most of the day. Audrey went to see the room which had a gorgeous view. He could see all the hills and mountains, flashes of green everywhere he looked. It was fit for a king. Very old fashion the floors and walls, but colorful.

He went back downstairs using the elevator that had to be decades old. There was a very rich sense of history. The building once held the people who worked in the tea fields. It hadn't been changed since then. The architecture held a central pit from which you could look down. The floors of the building were in a square shape at the center around the pit and extended to the sides, where the rooms were in a hall that were east and west. His parents had gone to their room to check the internet and were outside[2] on a grand balcony that looked over the hills.

"What a country." He thought.

There were tables arranged on the balcony which was a cool grey. Everything was white, the chairs and tables. They sat for a while basking in the fresh air and sun. High up in the hills, it was cooler now.

"Let's take some pictures." His father said.

---

2   In front of the building.

They stood up near the sides of the balcony and took photos. These would be the memories they would keep. One of the staff members told them there was a tour at 4 o' clock showing the way the tea is manufactured. Audrey wanted to see. He had no idea they would go to the fields and pick tea themselves. It was all a part of the tour they had. A lady placed a basket on his head with the handle facing backwards, resting on his back where the leaves would go. She showed him what to do. He could barely follow. She was so skilled and he was a novice. His parents came along and did the same thing. They were laughing. Ayomi the tour guide had given his mother a sari to wear and him and his father sarongs. It all felt so silly. Ayomi captured everything in pictures. Three of the worst tea pickers that ever lived.

"Let me get you putting the leaves in the basket." She said.

Audrey had a handful and raised his arms backward and completely missed.

"Nice job." His mom said.

That night they ate at the restaurant in the hotel where they were served every dish to their plate. Some of the food he had tried before, but it tasted different. Some of the dishes were new like the mango curry and pickled vegetables. They all went along with the rice that was the main base of the meal. Audrey left early so his parents could be alone. It had been a long day. As he laid in bed that night, he thought of what they did and smiled. He wouldn't take it for granted that his parents were healthy and so much a part of his life and this journey with each other.

SIMILE OF THE ELEPHANT'S FOOT

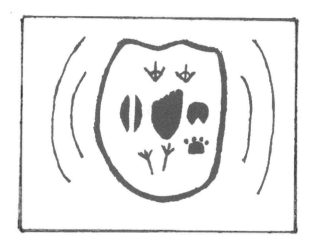

"In all my life, wherever I go, I have seen myself in others. Whatever color or shape, the way they talk or dress, I see myself. It's a blessing to have dealt with men like that, all I've seen, where every art was a connection, and every role I assumed was not my own, but theirs. My soul expands .... to contain them all." thought Audrey.

That morning they drove down from the tea estates. On the way they passed a waterfall and stopped by to see. Audrey photographed his mother and father together. There was peace between them. He didn't know how many more trips like this there would be. He looked out at the waterfall and thought how clear and pure it was, falling from a great height.

"Your majesty" he thought, "How beautiful."

Somehow it was enough, being there, seeing what nature could do. All his people, so happy all around him, like brothers and sisters, truly.

"This is where you came from." he thought as he rode in the van, "Never forget that."

So much had changed since the last time he was here. The small huts that people lived in were gone. It saddened him to see last time. Now there were houses and apartments, fine roads and highways, fast food places like America, anything you wanted. They were driving to a seaside town. There were beautiful coconut trees. They saw a temple nearby and went to see. They removed their shoes, their bare feet touched the ground where others stood, walking in silent prayer. The lord Buddha before them. It was years ago Audrey tried to reconcile what he had been taught as a child and the faith he found later, as a young adult. Somehow in his suffering the last few years he had lost his faith in part. Still he believed in God, in Buddha and what he taught, something higher that connects us, every one. It was for that he lived each day, to help and serve in whatever way he could. His grandma rose each day for that. It was all she had. In all we seek of meaning, it returns to faith and how we believe and how we live for the good of all. That's what matters. To treat each other kindly, to think clearly and soundly with good thoughts, to humble yourself, to live gracefully and accept and be aware, that life is something precious, to stand by truth, firm. That's the way, the middle path. Audrey got down on his knees and bowed.

"If only I would listen to what you said. It's never easy to be a good person. Every day I try. I'm tempted by things.

Desiring what I don't have, attached to all I do. There's so much to lose. I grow old. The people I love grow old too. I've learned to let go. I've paused for a moment, still I come back, wanting what I did before. I'm the same child I was before. Restless. Unhappy. Will I ever get better? I want to know. My experience has taught me some things in a different way, still I yield to you. You gave up everything for peace. I find it hard to do so. I'm holding on to something, I don't know what. I don't know why. I always will."

He watched his parents bow and waited.

"I wish I believed the way you do." He thought, "Without doubt. Even the Buddha had to find his own way. No one taught him."

They walked slowly to where they left their shoes. Seeing the Buddha like that was inspiring. There were many statues all throughout the country. When they bowed it was not for him, but what he taught. The way to freedom. Understanding. Known as enlightenment for those who practice. He could see they were happy and that alone brought him peace.

Soon they were back on the van.

"Remember the last time we were here we rode an elephant?" his mother asked.

How could he forget.

"Yeah, that was fun. It was you, me, and D. A little scary at first." Audrey said, "Was that your first time?"

"Yeah, it was the first time." She laughed, "I wanted something you could remember me by."

"I don't need an elephant to remember you. Just being here is enough. Riding with you and dad. It means a lot."

"I hope so." She smiled and then turned to look outside, "You never know how long or short life may be. "

She thought of her father and her sister, how suddenly they passed away. How it marked her life with fear and with sorrow. She never healed from them. To be here now was to relive so much.

She made a call to visit the school she attended when she was young. It was wonderful to retrace where she came from and how it all changed. A young teacher walked out to show them. For Audrey it was new. It was a school day like any other, the girls were in white. So beautiful and innocent. They walked along the gravel and saw the history there. Audrey didn't know what his mother felt, but he knew it was important to her. His father was there and walked peacefully. All the buildings were plain, mostly white, yet stylish in their simplicity. There were some benches outside to sit. The students were looking at these strange intruders. They respected them. Audrey smiled. They walked by the café where the students ate. It was after lunch by then. He peeked through the window at the small wooden tables that sat maybe twenty or thirty people in total. "I wonder how they all can eat." He said. They passed by the lecture hall for the older students that sat a hundred or more. It was fairly modern and very elegant with all the wood shining from the seats to the podium. They walked back out the front gate, said goodbye to the teacher, and took a photo.

"Another memory." He thought.

They boarded the van again. They drove for some time. Soon they arrived in a beautiful hotel by the ocean. He was met by his cousin Paul and his wife Yana and their son Aroon.

"Welcome back Audrey. It's been a while." Said Paul as he hugged him.

"Too long." Said Audrey.

"This is my wife Yana. You never met, and this little guy is Aroon."

"Nice to meet you all. I have so many questions to ask." Audrey laughed.

They stepped inside the hotel from the driveway that was in the front where they met. The hotel was open air to the back where the ocean kept turning. You could feel the breeze. They were greeted warmly and given their keys. Their bags were taken upstairs. Paul led them to the back where the ocean was only a few feet away. They stood by the water and spoke.

"I heard you graduated. Congratulations! We're so proud of you. That's what kept you away from us all this time. "

"I can't believe you have a kid now. He's so cute."

"Come here Aroon." Said Paul, motioning to his son.

Aroon ran and leapt up in his father's arms. The ocean noise playing in the background, the scent of the ocean lifted in the air, two cousins worlds apart now together, as the evening fell.

"He was waiting for you." Paul said as Aroon looked away, "No need to be shy now."

Audrey laughed.

"We have a small gift for you." He said to Aroon, "I'll show you later."

Audrey brushed his hand against his face. He was about three years old. So soft and cool. He had short black hair like his father, but his face was more like Yana. She stood a little distance from them, talking to his parents.

"How does it feel to be a dad?" Audrey asked smiling.

"Honestly, it's everything to me. It's what I always wanted. It's not easy some days. Some days I'm so busy, and then I come home and he wants to spend time. Yana works all day and comes home and has to cook. Her parents help. They watch him during the day. When I see the way he looks at me, how happy he is to be with me, what I struggled for all those years, it was worth it. There's a sense of attachment, that you made something, and you spend your life protecting it. You'll fall in love one day and you'll see. It's this connection, that no one can ever take from you. It's my family. It's deep and it's real, in a way that nothing else can be. This is love. One day you'll see."

"That's what I want Paul. Just the way you said."

They were silent for a while. Hearing the ocean, watching it recede.

"Let's get something to eat Audrey. There are others waiting. It's late now. We'll talk more then."

Audrey put his hand on Paul's shoulder, Aroon still carried by his father, they walked slowly back where his parents were talking. Yana looked at Audrey and smiled. He wondered what they told her. They went out to eat and came back late. He was so tired. Sleeping by the ocean that night, hearing the ocean as it gently turned, he slept as if he were a child again, as if every limb and bone were rested, in one night.

He didn't remember the last time he slept like that. What peace. He turned on his side, looking out at the ocean in a see through panel. The wall on his left was made of glass like a giant window that showed the whole view. He stood up and pressed his hand against it. What a sight to behold.

He sat down and wrote his thoughts. He looked at the unmade bed, a beautiful net pulled to the side right above, the white sheets, the wooden frame, handsomely built, and he thought how lucky he was to have it all.

It was his last day on the island and he still hadn't seen Sohan and his sister Sara. Sara had two kids Lyla and Siddarth. Lyla was seven and Siddharth was five. Lyla had a slight case of autism. She was very sweet. When they arrived she ran up and down full of excitement. When they opened the door she took Audrey's hand and stroked it as if he were a prince.

"My beautiful uncle." She said, "My beautiful uncle. I'm so happy to see you."

Audrey was taken back. He didn't feel he deserved to be treated with such respect. He looked at her face, how innocent and well meaning she was. She clapped her hands in joy.

"Come sit uncle. Please sit."

It broke his heart to see her this way, in the best way. She wore a beautiful dress that was purple with a little white flower on the chest. She was laughing the whole time.

"We have gifts too." Audrey's father said.

He handed her a bag that was for her and Siddharth. She pulled out a lovely backpack that was pink with a bright rainbow on the top. Siddarth pulled out a Superman doll.

"Do you like it?" his father asked her.

"I love it." She said, "Thank you so much."

She ran and showed her mom.

"Look what they gave me." She said.

"I know. I see. Very nice. You can take it to school tomorrow." Replied Sara.

"Thank you uncle." She said again.

Siddarth was too busy playing with the toy. He was very happy.

"What do you say, Siddarth?" asked Sara.

"Thank you." He said and ran away again.

"I'll make some tea." Said Sohan.

They sat and talked. They hadn't seen each other in seventeen years. Sara was just a child then. It was a brand new house and the high spirit of reunion was in the air. Everyone was cheerful. They were happy and healthy, all of them. The elders and the young. It was a new generation full of hope of what could be. They were blessed to have each other in one moment they would always remember. Being so near after years apart.

Sohan came with the tea in a silver tray. He placed it on the table.

"So Audrey, what's new? How's your trip been?" he asked very politely as he always did.

"It's been wonderful. It seemed like only a few days. I lost sense of time. We saw all the family. That was the best part. We drove around for days, taking everything in. We stopped here and there. What I feel I feel inside. It's hard to explain. I've seen so many places in my life, but this is home. More than the tea estates or the ocean or whatever else I saw I feel complete. This land, these people, make me whole. They're in me, and I'm in them, and it all feels right. Our people."

"It's nice to hear you say that. We missed you. Last time you were here we had such a great time. When you were gone it wasn't the same. We saw your pictures, but it's not the same. To hear your voice, the way you laugh, to see you in person, was what we all needed. Especially Sara. She missed you so much. She thought about you the whole time. "

Audrey looked at her. She smiled.

"It's true." She said.

Audrey looked at Sohan. To him he would always be that young boy, who spoke little but felt greatly, very patient. He was strong, he didn't need anyone and yet he loved his family and had a strong sense of duty. He would guard them always.

Sara went to put away the tea. They spoke for a while, reminiscing. They lost track of time. Audrey played with Siddarth as Lyla helped Sara. They brought out the food. It was string hoppers with shrimp and gravy, lentils, fried onions, coconut, everything they could ask for. They ate till they were full. With a full belly he could sleep well. He thanked them for what they gave. They talked a little more until it was late. Lyla wanted them to stay, of course they couldn't.

She said, "Thank you uncle for coming. Thank you for the backpack."

She hugged them. Siddarth had gone to sleep. They went outside and said goodbye.

"Please come back, anytime." Sara said. They bowed to his parents. What a beautiful night it was. Audrey looked back at them and what they shared and how they made each other feel.

"I never felt so respected." He thought as he left.

They went to say goodbye to his grandma who lived nearby. They bowed one last time. They were grateful to see each other. Audrey's mother said a few words. Audrey thought about living without his mother. How hard it must be. He knew she was sad to go. They didn't know if they would see each other again. Wasn't it scary? They went on the van and headed for the airport. As they drove late that night, Audrey thought about all he saw. The rich and the poor, the beautiful estates and the people who lived without basic living, the children without shoes, the mothers without doctors in need of healthcare, the government buildings, the temples of ancient time, the commerce, the culture, the streets busy in the day, all the colors bursting, the people in the fields and the people in the market, all united, singing as one. He looked out his window at a young girl who smiled as he went. Unaware of a life beyond this place. Everything she had was enough.

"This is where you came from." He thought to himself, "Never forget that."

LOVE AS THOUGH THE TIME WOULD BE
(WAITING FOR YOU)

One day when the sky was deep blue, Audrey flew away to see Mary. The house was no longer lopsided, but tall and straight. There was a garden out front, the grass was trim. Everywhere you looked there were flowers and beautiful colors all about. As he stepped to the house the path was clean. He knocked on the door. Mary came out surprised, but fully radiant as if the sun had come out startled by the earth. Her honey-brown hair swept to the side, as she touched her neck.

"Audrey, it's you! What are you doing here?! Please come in." said Mary as she hugged him, "I thought I'd never see you again."

Mary had a pink blouse with tight black pants and Audrey was in a orange shirt with blue lines in a cross pattern and dark jeans.

"You know I couldn't stay away," he smiled as he walked in, "Where's little Dominic?"

"He's not so little anymore." She laughed, "He's at school. He'll be eight soon. They grow up so fast."

"I'm not sure if he remembers me. He was so quiet back then."

"He talks much more these days. I think he'll be happy to see you. I've told him about you, how you saved me, not once but twice. You're the reason we got the house back. I'm so grateful for everything you did. I really am."

Audrey noticed an older man's hat and jacket on the coat rack.

"Is someone here?" he asked.

"No, that's just Liam's. I forgot to tell you. I met someone." She said beaming, "He's amazing. He's everything I was looking for. I'll tell you all about him. We have some catching up to do. Are you hungry? I can make a sandwich."

"That sounds pretty good." He said.

They went to the breakfast table and he sat down as Mary opened the fridge to get the food out.

"You like turkey?" she asked.

"Perfect."

She fixed the sandwich and set it out before him.

"You eat, I'll talk," She laughed, "So when you left me and Dominic had to rebuild our life together. I had the house worked up. It wasn't easy and it took some time. Little by little things got back to normal. I started going to church again. Everyone was so kind. They brought us food and chipped in with donations and help around the house. I was lucky to have them. They knew all about me, ever since I was a kid. My mother worked for the church for a long time. She had so many friends. I trusted them. After we settled down they said it was time for me to find someone. They knew a young man named Liam who moved here recently. I saw him a few times before he introduced himself. I thought he was handsome. I knew when I touched his hand that there was something. He was strong but when he held my hand he was soft and when I looked in his eyes I felt safe. He had a quiet dignity and a warmth in his presence. It just felt right. At first we talked here and there. After Ham, I didn't want to rush anything. He understood. I think he heard about me through all the ladies. One day one of the newlyweds had a small party at her house. She invited all the couples she knew as well as Liam and I. We sat down on the couch and talked, sipping wine.

He told me he was looking for friends, that he was busy with work. He had a small accounting practice and was picking up clients. He said he was single. He had been engaged to his longtime girlfriend who changed her mind when she met a young lawyer at work one day. He wasn't able to provide the life she wanted. It was a hard loss and he hadn't dated for years. He needed a fresh start so he moved here. He said it was scary but exciting. We went out on a date after that. We were both nervous. The two of us went to see a movie. He came to pick me up and he had a gift for Dominic. He spoils him with all these toys. Dominic loves him. He was the father figure he never had, that I hope he has. After that there were more dates. I fell in love complete-ly. I didn't believe it, that a man so good could still be out there. I wondered if there was anything wrong that I didn't know. He was mature and smart and sensitive. We under-stood each other's past and from that our love grew. Before I met him, I convinced myself I was too old to be in love again. That I would be alone for the rest of my life and that was okay. I feel so blessed to have a second chance. I never thought I'd meet someone like him, so honest and true."

Audrey looked at the ring on her finger. She noticed him.

"It's true. I'm engaged. I don't think I've ever been this happy. I want you to meet him."

"I'm so happy for you. If anyone deserves a married life it's you. You're wiser now. I trust you. If you say he's the one, I believe you."

"It's like we're the same soul, him and I. I never felt that way before, that someone was out there and we were meant to be together."

"I know you wouldn't jeopardize Dominic like that."

"That's the thing Audrey. They love each other. You have to see the way they are with each other. We're a family now. It's all of us. Me, Liam, Dominic. This is what I always pictured it would be. This is real."

"I'm glad."

"What about you? How is everything?"

"I wish I had something new to say. I was busy with school. I guess I can say I'm a doctor now. I'm on a break at the moment. I haven't started working yet. It's been a long road. I see a light somewhere. Recently I've been going here and there. I saw my family who I haven't seen in years. It was really nice."

"That's amazing! A doctor. You act like it's no big deal. That's what you've been doing all these years. We have to celebrate."

"I'm too old for that."

"There's no such thing. At least come for the wedding."

"If you want me to. I'll be there. "

"It would mean a lot. I can't believe it. A doctor. You're always so secretive. Have you met a girl yet?"

"I have friends but nothing serious. There's this girl Teller. I've known her since I was a kid. I never really know how I feel about her. Somedays I feel it's love, other days it's more like friendship. She's incredible in every way. She's smart, she's kind, she's beautiful. I just don't know if she's the one. I have to follow my gut feeling. I always feel like there's someone out there, I haven't met them. Someone like you and Liam, waiting for me. It's hard to explain."

"I think I understand. You'll know it when you find it. Love is a great mystery, magical, beyond science. You feel your way through."

"I also feel I'm wasting time though. I'm getting older. I'm tired of waiting. I feel like I'm in the air, floating, going nowhere. I've always been a long term person, planning ahead. Now I just don't know and it's so hard for me."

"I've felt that way before. It's scary. I wish I had nice words to say that would make it better. You have to trust yourself. Take whatever steps you can. Put yourself out there. Meet people. Use your friends. You'll find someone and when you know, you'll know for sure."

Just then, there was a rustling at the door and little Dominic was in tears.

"What's the matter?" she asked him.

Dominic was surprised to see Audrey and he felt more embarrassed to be crying.

'The kids at school. It's always the same."

MIXTAPE

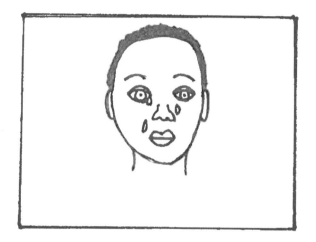

"Dominic, this is Audrey. Remember I told you about him?" said Mary.

"Nice to meet you." He said in between sobbing.

"What's all this crying about?" she asked.

"Remember John. I thought he was my friend, but he didn't invite me for his birthday. It's a sleepover. I asked him why. He said the other kids didn't want me there."

"Why is that?" she asked.

"It's this one kid Max who calls me dirty. Now the other kids are following. They said it's my skin. They don't want to play with anyone with mixed blood."

"It shouldn't matter what you look like."

"I told you about this before."

"You have to be nice to them." She said.

"I'm nice to everyone. They're not nice to me." Said Dominic raising his voice.

"What else did they do?" she asked.

"One girl said my hair is ugly. The other kids said my nose is too wide. They laugh at me behind my back. I told you that."

"I'm sorry Dom. There's no excuse for that."

"Some of them act like they like me, but they don't want to sit with me. I thought John was my friend, but he didn't even invite me."

"Maybe there were too many people."

"It's their parents. They don't like me either."

"I'm not sure what to do. I can talk to your teacher tomorrow. I know it's hard for you."

"Some of them are jealous because I'm the best student in class and they chose me to be the lead in the school play this year."

"You're a great student, I know that. I'm so proud of you. You work so hard."

"They don't like when I get so much attention."

"I understand."

"Don't let people like that get to you Dom. I hope you don't mind me saying." Audrey chimed in, "Don't let anyone make you feel like you're not good enough. I remember when I was younger people used to tease me about everything. I don't think there was one feature on my face they didn't pull apart. I felt terrible. I couldn't even look in the mirror. I hated myself. They made me hate myself. For the longest time I really believed I was the only one with something wrong with me. There are so many differences in the way people look. As you get older you embrace those things. All those things you thought were 'wrong' are really the best thing about you. You're special. Don't let anyone take that away from you."

"Thanks Audrey." Said Mary, "I agree. You're special Dom. I love you, and he loves you, and so does Liam. We're here for you, always. I just wanted to say how brave you are for telling me Dom. I know it's not easy. It was very mature of you. Now we can do something."

"Just don't embarrass me at school in front of people. It's hard enough as it is."

"I understand and I won't do that."

"She's got your back Dom." Audrey said.

Mary gave Dominic a big hug.

"Are you hungry?" she asked.

"No I got homework to do." He said, "I'll eat when Liam gets back."

Dominic went upstairs and Mary and Audrey talked. The time went by and soon it was evening. The door turned again and this time it was Liam. He smiled at both of them. He had short brown hair spiked upwards in the front, and a small, thick mustache. He wasn't very tall but he had broad shoulders and wore a white dress shirt with a black tie. Mary introduced the two of them.

"This is Audrey," She said, "and Audrey this is Liam."

Audrey stood up and shook his hand. It only took a few minutes to remove any doubts Audrey had about him. He was reserved but cheerful, he had a deep voice that shook sometimes as if he were uncertain. He spoke and listened equally. It didn't take long before they talked about Dominic. Liam was sad to hear.

"I remember when I was younger I struggled with my weight. The children would tease me. They shouted names from the window when I was at recess. I had friends and they were nice, but I always had that fear that someone would make fun of me in front of everyone. I was shy and I didn't speak much. I thought if I could just stay away from the spotlight I wouldn't be insulted. In high school I had a girlfriend, I started working out. I was more outgoing and a lot slimmer. She was in the marching band so I joined as a drummer. I was the happiest I'd been. I wanted to stay together when we were in college but she broke up with me. She said she wanted to see other people. That's when I crashed again. I tried to eat away my sorrow. Everywhere I went I thought about her, how much she meant to me. It was hard. When I ate I thought about her, when I slept I thought about her. I had all our pictures and I would look at them all the time. It only made it worse. I was obsessed. When you fall in love the first time, it's like that. I gained so much weight. I felt ashamed to walk out the door. Everyone was looking at me. None of my clothes fit. I felt like a freak. I felt guilty and sad. My friends tried to help but I wouldn't listen. I had to get counseling and I signed up with a trainer to get back on my feet. I never wanted to feel that way again.

Life breaks you in so you can hold love proper. Now I know what it is to love. Life will humble even the greatest men. That's the way it should be. We all have to learn sometime. It's the human experience. It makes us better people."

"I agree." said Audrey, "Thanks for sharing."

"Dominic will be alright. He's a strong kid. We'll talk to his teacher though, see what she can do." Said Liam.

Just then Dominic walked down. He knew they were talking about him and his ears grew hot.

"Hey Liam." He said shyly.

"Hey Dom. I heard you had a hard day at school today. Sorry to hear. We'll talk later, you and I."

"I haven't made anything for dinner." Said Mary.

"I'll buy something." Said Liam.

"I'm sure you're busy these days planning the wedding." Said Audrey steering the conversation away.

"Everything has to be right" she smiled.

"Hey Audrey." Said Dominic.

"Yeah Dom."

"Thanks for everything."

"You're coming for the wedding, right?" asked Liam.

"How could I turn it down? I've been waiting for this." Replied Audrey with a warm look at Mary.

Mary stood up and went to the sink.

"It just gets better and better." She said with a big smile on her face.

WEDDING DAY

Picking a suit for the wedding was easy. He only had one. It was royal blue that he wore with a red tie and white shirt. He had a red pocket square to match. The night before the wedding he tried the suit on. It was a little big. He had lost weight recently as he increased his running speed and switched to a protein shake in the morning before exercise. He would be fine. It was better to save money rather than spending it on something that was only one day.

"There might be other weddings in the future," he said to himself, "I'll worry about that later."

He looked at himself in the mirror. He liked what he saw. A young man, a gentleman. All he ever wanted he had become. He was handsome and strong. There was a brightness that radiated from his eyes. He was self-assured but grounded in faith. He knew his own shortcomings yet he understood his worth. He had studied hard for so many years and he could see it on his face and the way he carried himself. It was natural. Everything he did he meant well for his health and the benefit of others. He had little imperfections and flaws in character, yet he hoped to be forgiven. Where he had acted wrong and misspoken he would always remember. Someway he would try to correct himself. It was all he could do. He was a cautious man who thought long and hard before he did anything, yet he still made mistakes and that was okay. As a whole he was pure and that was rare.

On the day of the wedding he put on his suit and went outside waiting for the wind to pick up. He flew near the park where the wedding would be with a gift under his arm. He straightened his tie as he put away his umbrella. He walked to a beautiful gazebo with white pillars with white bars around the bottom and a grey roof. There were trees all around. Inside the gazebo was a cello player and three violins setting up for the ceremony. They were dressed in all black. The two men played violin in suits with purple ties. The ladies, one blonde and one brunette, played cello and violin. They were quietly talking. Audrey placed his gift down on a big table off to the side where the guests were coming in. There were ladies from the church who were close to Mary and friends of Liam. There was a young couple who Audrey spoke with. The gentleman knew Liam for years. He said they grew up together. His name was George and his wife Luann. They talked about themselves for a while.

"How do you know Mary?" she asked.

"It was years ago. I found her in the woods. She was lost. I walked her home. We were kids. You should have seen her mother. It was such a relief to have her back." He smiled, but he wasn't sure if he was happy or sad, "A few years later I found her again. I was able to help her with something and I met Dominic. We only knew each other briefly. There were lifetimes between us though. It's what she meant to me. She was like family. She still is."

Speaking these words, it suddenly occurred to him that he still had feelings for her. What was he to do with them? He would always love her. They weren't quiet feelings either. They were present and real. He continued speaking, yet his mind was elsewhere. There was always some part of him that felt like she was his. To watch her get married to someone else was to lose her again. Why now? Why all of this again, at this moment that was supposed to be hers? It wasn't fair to speak out. Not now. It was too late, or was it? Should he say something? What would that do?

He excused himself and walked to a secluded spot. His hand ran back to the hair by his neck and then down again into his pocket, very slowly. He looked out at the trees and thought about all he left behind. His whole life. How many girls did he let slip away. When she was single there was the possibility. To hand her off to someone was to let that flame expire.

"Was there anyone out there for him?" he thought to himself.

He had to know. He was tired of playing the fool. How helpless he felt, yet he had to be strong. Today was Liam's day. He was there for her, when Audrey couldn't be. She said herself, they were soulmates. Who was he to do anything now?

One of the guests came and said the ceremony was about to start. When Audrey walked back the music was playing and down in pairs the groomsmen walked down the aisles. They all wore black suits with a bowtie. They all looked happy. Next the bridesmaids came down and settled to the side of the gazebo opposite the groomsmen. The music played off to the side of the guests where they had moved from before. There were no seats for the guests. Everyone was standing. The music continued as Liam came down the aisle with his parents. His hair and mustache neatly trimmed. He and his father in black and his mother in burgundy. It was great to see them.

Out of the corner of his eye Audrey saw the farmer he had met so many years ago, who helped Mary. His hair was gone now, but he looked quite elegant as he was composed. They quietly acknowledged each other. Very soon the bride was walking down the aisle as the music played. There was little Dominic walking beside her. Her hair was a darker shade of brown. His heart sunk, but soon revived. Watching her, so graceful and really beaming with pride, he knew this was the right choice. He saw Liam stunned by her beauty. They had both failed in love and now were marked with joy. It was no small comfort to have found each other. They were both lucky, very equally so.

They both exchanged vows.

"I never thought I'd be so lucky to find someone and then I met you. You changed my life completely. I was alone for so long. You filled my life with everything I ever sought. A family. I'll always work to make you happy. I'll be faithful and I'll be true. I promise to the end, I'll be there. We'll lean upon each other, as they say in the Bible, it takes two. Where I fall you'll pick me up, and where you need me I'll be waiting, always. I only want you for the rest of my life. It's you. Forever, you and I." the groom said.

"For so long I didn't know what I deserved. What love could be. You showed me what it means to really be in love. It goes both ways and it's powerful. It makes me stronger every day. I'm so blessed to have you, I always will be. You've given me and Dominic the family we always wanted. I hope that we can stay this way forever. Whatever comes, we'll face it together. This is us now, you and me. We'll never be alone again, no matter what, we'll always have each other. That means everything to me. You are my person, my soulmate, my love."

With that the ceremony continued.

"Do you take this woman to be your lawfully wedded wife?" asked the pastor.

"I do." Said Liam.

"And do you take this man to be your lawfully wedded husband?"

"I do." She said.

"By the power vested in me, I now pronounce you man and wife. You may now kiss the bride."

Liam drew the veil and kissed her deeply, passionately. Everyone cheered. Audrey was happy too. He loved her so. They made their way down the aisle together as the music played. Flowers were thrown. They stepped in a car off to the reception. Liam's mother had tears in her eyes as she watched her son go by. She had wanted this for so many years. The guests soon dispersed.

The day continued with the whole group dancing and drinking in the reception hall. It was a very different kind of music playing now. Pictures were taken and speeches were given. Audrey sat down and took it all in. He didn't know anyone at his table. He saw a beautiful redhead sitting by herself. She was on the other side of the dancefloor. She was one of the bridesmaids in light pink. He drank his gin and tonic and went over.

"Hi, my name's Audrey. I saw you at the wedding. You look beautiful. How do you know Mary?"

"Thanks. We're old friends. I went to high school with her. You look pretty sharp yourself." She smiled.

"Would you like to dance with me?"

She looked down at her phone.

"I have a boyfriend." She said.

"I see. I was just wondering." Said Audrey a little embarrassed now, "I hope you have fun."

He walked back to his table and sat there a little shamefully. It's never easy to ask someone to dance. At least he tried. As you get older you're less afraid. Not knowing is worse than trying. He spoke with some of the men at the table. He shared his experience and laughed. On the dancefloor people were dancing their hearts out. The women were turning, spinning around. The men had their hands in the air.

"I might as well join them" Audrey said.

He took off his jacket and felt his legs unwind, playing with the rhythm. His arms swayed to the music that filled the room. He forgot all his cares for a while. Shuffling his feet, dancing about. He was happy. He looked at everyone and they were all the same, celebrating. He spotted Liam and Mary talking to the guests. He kept dancing as if he had lost himself completely. It was the best time. He was free.

Soon the food was served. He ran into Mary and Liam and said, "Congratulations!" Mary had changed from before. She was in a beautiful orange dress. She never looked better.

"I'm so happy for both of you. He's the perfect guy for you, and you're the perfect girl for him. It's really meant to be."

"Thanks. We're so glad you're here." Said Mary.

He took her hand and squeezed it gently.

"I wouldn't miss it for anything."

"Oh, there's someone I want you to meet. This is my friend Lauren from the church. I told her about you. She's single. She graduated recently. She's very smart like you." Mary smiled.

"It's nice to meet you." Said Audrey as he shook her hand. "Would you like to dance a little bit later? After we eat. I'll find you."

"I'd be honored." She said.

The night went on and Audrey saw Lauren. They talked a little and danced a lot more. She was young with blonde hair and brown eyes. She had a black dress and quite the form. They felt like kids again. She knew how to dance and they mouthed the words to every song. It felt good to have someone, even if he'd never see her again. Laughing through the night, sharing the joy in the crowd, being there, it was all for Mary. He had known her better than most. He had seen her in her weakest moment and that's why he loved her more. He was her guardian, but now Liam was to be the one. He felt himself grow smaller, as if the place he occupied was gone. He would still be her friend and she needed that. It was bittersweet. Dancing there, he danced for her. It was all he could do.

CHOOSE YOUR BATTLE

Mary and Liam were leaving for their honeymoon and Audrey volunteered to stay with Dominic for a few days. Every day they went for a walk down a sandy road and near the woods. Dominic would get home from school and they would go. On the fourth day they stopped by a white fence to get some rest. The fence belonged to a house nearby. There was a large rock and a smaller one side by side. They were the perfect seats. All around them were fields of grass and homes here and there.

"It's a beautiful day." said Audrey as he sat down, leaning on the bigger one.

"Yeah it is, but for some reason I just don't feel right." Said Dominic as he sat beside him on the rock that was about two feet high.

"What's the matter?"

"I don't want to go to school anymore."

"Why not? Is it the other kids?"

"It's more than that. I just don't see the point. Why can't I just stay home?"

"There's a lot you can learn from school. Right now you're starting a foundation and as you get older you'll build upon it. You have to learn the basics first. Reading and writing, math, science, and history. It's so much fun. Think of them as little blocks of knowledge. At first it's scary, cause you don't know what you're building. You have to trust your parents and your teachers. One day you realize what you want to do and then you start shaping it the way you want. You add the blocks you want and design something truly amazing. It's your career, your life, all that you decide."

He looked at Dominic to see how he felt.

"I have no idea what I want to do."

"And that's the fun part. You're still young. We all have a purpose. It's not clear sometimes. We have to trust ourselves to find it. It takes longer for some people, and that's okay. You may live a quarter of your life, and realize what you're doing is wrong. You still have that foundation. You adapt and change and keep building. I was lucky. I knew what I wanted to do since I was a kid. My father was sick when I was young. I wanted to take care of him. I had to do that. I didn't have a choice. That's the way I felt. I was compelled. I had to learn everything about medicine so I could help my father. That would help me and my mother too. I wanted to help other people who were the same. Health is so important. It's so exciting too. I loved learning about the human body, how it all works, every molecule, every reaction and process, every organ and every system. I wanted to dedicate my life to that. That was me. For you it may be something completely different. You might have an experience that changes the way you see things. You might discover something that fascinates you endlessly. You'll want to spend your whole life doing that. Whatever you love, do that. Whatever you care about. Find it. Never stop looking. Think about your future, the practical side, how do you make a living, how do you stay passionate, what do you want to do. Nobody can tell you but yourself. For some people just being a parent is enough. Having a family and taking care of them. Some people are born with a drive to do great things. They may care for the welfare of people and study the law or serve the country. Some might fight in the military because that's what they were meant to do. Firefighters and policemen, construction workers, teachers who don't get the credit they deserve, we need all of them. You have to choose what battle you fight. Everyone's good at something. You have to dedicate the time and effort to succeed. To be the best at something it has to come from within. Weigh everything, see every side. Be mindful of the life you want. It's up to you."

"I know. It's not that I'm bad at school either, I do well. It's just some days I don't want to be there."

"When I was in high school I had terrible anxiety. Just sitting around was torture, being around other people. I looked at my calendar and saw all the days that were left, and I was filled with such dread I could feel the weight of my heart depress. I was mortified. I had no idea what was wrong with me or why I felt the way I did. Honest to God, I don't know how I made it through. I think for me I didn't feel I had a choice. All my friends went to school, that was expected of me too. What else would I do? When you say that you're scared, I know how you feel, believe me. That's why religion is so important. You have to believe in something higher than yourself. Always work for God, for the good of all people. If you're good at school, use that good for something. Don't waste your life. Someway, give it meaning. You're here for some reason. It's more than you think."

"You really believe that?" asked Dominic.

"Of course I do. I wouldn't say it otherwise. I put my faith in you."

"I guess mom would be unhappy if I quit."

"Of course she would. You're still young Dominic, there's a whole world out there you don't know. It's exciting. I can't wait to see what you grow up to be. You'll have to work hard, incredibly hard sometimes, that goes without saying. If you work continuously, with patience and due diligence, there's nothing you can't do. Always be truthful and moderate. You'll succeed. All you need is already inside of you. God will do the rest. Trust in him. Keep building. Never stop."

Dominic just shook his head as if he understood. He broke the silence.

"Thanks for everything you told me. I appreciate it."

Audrey went up to Dominic and gave him a hug. He held him tight.

"You know I love you Dom. I always will."

The two of them walked back home, over the grass, with new hopes and a bright outlook as if it were the start of something new. The sun would be out tomorrow. It would be another day, where they would be fine. Liam and Mary would be back soon. It seemed like everything was waiting, the house, the child, the perfect union.

HOW TO BREATHE

There's a story, and if you follow it right,
Good things will come.
The way of life as written by God.
How we begin, how we die
Suffer some, love and marry.
It brings peace to the mind.

"I'm not afraid to stand alone. I've made it this far. If there's someone out there, I'll meet her. One day. These days I drive at night looking for something. It feels good just to turn the car on and go. I work out, I study, I sleep with no one there. I have my family though. That's enough for now. Looking back at my life, all I ever wanted was control. When my father was ill, I lost that. As I learned I regained that sense, and as I drive, I've somehow come back to who I am. My hands are on the wheel. All the knowledge I gained was to make the world a better place. Wherever I go tonight is my choice to make.

I see the road before me. It's dark, my lights are on. The streets are mostly empty. So much of the world depends on what we do. I believe in free will. I'm starting to believe in myself again, how my mother always did. Her faith has guided me. Where I doubted myself, she led me forward to try. Now I steer for both of us. Any turn I make is the right one.

I remember when I was younger, I helped my mom back out of the parking lot. I stood on my knees looking out the back window. She was afraid. 'It's safe mom' I said and she trusted me. Now we're all safe. We made it somehow." thought Audrey.

"If there's anything to learn from the last few years, it's how patient I've been. I see myself, having succeeded a great deal, on one side, waiting to help the others over. I have no pride, only the right kind. I wish the best for everyone. I've always had that spirit, ever since I was a kid. I count that as the better part of me. I'm grown now, I certainly don't look the same. Time has done its work on me, inside and out. I feel changed. There's a wisdom I've gained, a boldness and clarity from all my mistakes.

As I drive alone, I see the cars pass me by and I feel the buzz of their speed. There is so much out there. There is so much more we imagine than what we see. In our dreams I feel the infinite, waiting for me to compose. I have set a chain which binds the night to me. I have lifted off. I am not afraid to stand alone. I am the creator of everything I see and whatever street I turn, rises to me, only to collapse when I go. Folding, receding when I look back. This is the world I live. I keep driving, almost praying, to find the meaning for every day, and every breath that God has given.

EPILOGUE

"I've always been a solitary person. I feel I owe something to someone. You never know unless you try." thought Audrey as he reached for his phone.

"Hey Teller. It's Audrey. I was wondering if you'd like to go out some time, as boyfriend and girlfriend?"

"I would love to."

"It's just …. "

"I would love to."

Thanks to everyone who helped in the making of this book.
Every reader.

Milton Keynes UK
Ingram Content Group UK Ltd.
UKHW050806201123
432900UK00011B/241

SAY AUDREY II